Kyle
on
4th
B'day
May 14, 1992
from
"Me-Maw"

BUZZLE BILLY

A BOOK ABOUT
SHARING

Michael P. Waite
Illustrated by Jill Colbert Trousdale

Chariot Books
DAVID C. COOK PUBLISHING CO.

To my parents, Richard and Margaret Waite,
for defining love as a way of life. *MPW*

To the humans of Hoomania. *JCT*

Chariot Books is an imprint of David C. Cook Publishing Co.
David C. Cook Publishing Co., Elgin, Illinois 60120
David C. Cook Publishing Co., Weston, Ontario

BUZZLE BILLY

© 1987 by Michael P. Waite for text and illustrations

Cover design by Dawn Lauck
First printing, 1987
Printed in the United States of America
92 91 90 89 88 5 4 3 2

Library of Congress Cataloging-in-Publication Data
Waite, Michael P., 1960-
    Buzzle Billy.
    (Building Christian character series)
    Summary: When Buzzle Billy stops sharing, Gimme Hands pop out of his sides and no one wants to play with him
anymore.
    [1. Sharing—Fiction. 2. Christian life—Fiction. 3. Stories in rhyme]
I. Trousdale, Jill, ill. II. Title. III. Series: Waite, Michael P., 1960-   . Building Christian character series.
PZ8.3.W136Bu 1987   [E]   87-5282
ISBN 1-55513-218-9

Dear Mom and Dad,

   Did you ever hide your child's pill in a spoonful of jelly? That's how the lesson about sharing is tucked into *Buzzle Billy*. The teaching is couched in a fun, rhyming story.

   You and your children can't help but smile at Buzzle Billy and his "Gimme Hands." But there's no missing his message: Sharing is right and important.

   How can you use this book to help train your children?

   Read Buzzle Billy aloud, as a family. Talk about the story and why sharing is important for God's children. Discuss Hebrews 13:16, the verse found on page 31, and memorize it together. The verse will serve as a reminder of the Christian character trait of sharing.

   Use catch words from the story to remind each other of the lesson: "Remember the Gimme Hands" may become your family's code for "remember to share."

   Young readers will enjoy reading the book to themselves and to their younger brothers and sisters. Nonreaders can tell themselves the story by looking at the pictures after it's been read aloud a couple of times.

   Building Christian character is hard work—but it can be done in an enjoyable way, as *Buzzle Billy* points out.

Buzzle Billy was a Buzzle,
Buzzles had a land of puzzles!

All the houses, schools, and stores,
Had puzzle walls and puzzle floors.
Buzzles made them all that way
'Cause best of all, they liked to play!

And Buzzles knew that playing fair
Meant that they must learn to share.
So, Buzzle Billy learned one day
How sharing was a part of play.

7

He played with other girls and boys,
He shared his paints and books and toys.
What fun he had with all his friends!
He thought that it would never end.

8

They rode Buzz-carts,
They played Buzz-darts,
They went on hikes,
They rode their bikes,
And on and on and on they played
'Til something happened one sad day!

9

Buzzle Billy saw a boy
Playing with his favorite toy!
"That's mine," he shouted. "Gimme that!"
He pushed the boy and took it back.

Something awful happened next—
Something you would not expect!
A hand popped out of Billy's side.
"Look!" the other Buzzles cried.
But Billy did not understand . . .
He had a case of GIMME HANDS.

POP!

When Buzzles turned to selfishness,
It got them in an awful mess,
Each time they reached for something new,
POP! A brand-new hand just grew!

"This is strange!" young Billy thought.
But still it didn't make him stop.
Another hand would be a help!
So Billy grabbed for something else.

And when he did, a fourth hand grew—
Now that was something very new!
The more he grabbed, the more hands grew.
He now had ten instead of two!
He grabbed and nabbed up all the toys,
He took them all and laughed with joy!

Then all the children ran away.
Without their toys, they could not play. . . .
Those Gimme Hands made them afraid.
See what trouble Billy made?

Now Buzzle Billy laughed with glee,
"All these toys belong to me!
They are mine! I will not share!
Mine! Mine! Mine! I won't play fair!"

Now that all his friends were gone
Buzzle Billy sat alone.
He sat and played all by himself,
All alone . . .
With no one else.
And soon he thought, "This is no fun,
I need a friend; I'll go find one.
I'll make a friend, but I won't share.
I'll keep my toys, and they'll keep theirs!"

He saw some Buzzles playing ball,
"Hello! May I play, too?" he called.
They turned and looked . . .
And saw his hands!
All those hands!
Those Gimme Hands!

And then they turned around and ran.
"He's got Gimme Hands!" they cried.
"He'll take our toys. . . . Let's run and hide!"

Soon all the Buzzle kids were gone,
And Buzzle Billy stood alone.
"This is no fun at all!" he moaned.
"It's no fun to play alone.
But I won't share!"

"I will NOT!
I won't give up the toys I've got!"

But everywhere he looked for friends,
Buzzles shouted, "Gimme Hands!"
They shouted, then they ran away,
So Billy had no place to play.

Biking Buzzles rode away,

19

Go-cart Buzzles drove away,

Boating Buzzles rowed away,
Those Buzzles simply would not stay.
When Billy came the others ran.
They ran off shouting, "Gimme Hands!"

And on it went for days and days,
All alone poor Billy played.
How he missed his Buzzle friends!
Why did all those good times end?

Then as he sat alone and cried,
A Buzzle girl came from behind.
She saw poor Billy all alone
And asked him, "Is there something wrong?"
"Yes!" said Billy. "Something's wrong!
All my Buzzle friends are gone."

"Everyone has run away
And there is no one left to play.
I have Gimme Hands, you see,
So everyone's afraid of me!
What an awful thing I've done!
I didn't know what I'd begun."
He bawled and sobbed and looked so sad,
The Buzzle girl felt very bad.

"I will play with you," said she.
"But only if you'll share with me.
I sure do like your teddy bear,
That's a toy that you could share!"

Buzzle Billy looked surprised.
He wiped the tears out of his eyes.
"You'll be my friend? Will you really?
Then I will share!" cried Buzzle Billy.
He handed her the teddy bear
With button eyes and fluffy hair.

And can you guess what happened then?
Guess what happened to that hand!
One Gimme Hand just disappeared,
And Buzzle Billy jumped and cheered.
For now he knew why they were there—
All because he did not share.

POOF!

So then he shouted very loud,
He shouted 'til he had a crowd.
"Come here Buzzle girls and boys!
Who would like to share my toys?"

The more he shared, the more they cheered,
His Gimme Hands all disappeared!
The Buzzle children laughed and played
And many, many friends were made.

29

For boys and girls who like to share
Will find a friend most anywhere!

And do not forget to do good and to share with others, for with such sacrifices God is pleased.

Hebrews 13:16 (NIV)

Look for all the great stories in the
Building Christian Character series

Buzzle Billy—A Book About Sharing
Handy-Dandy Helpful Hal—A Book About Helpfulness
Miggy and Tiggy—A Book About Overcoming Jealousy
Suzy Swoof—A Book About Kindness
Max and the Big Fat Lie—A Book About Telling the Truth
Casey the Greedy Young Cowboy—A Book About Being Thankful
Sir Maggie the Mighty—A Book About Obedience
Boggin, Blizzy, and Sleeter the Cheater—A Book About Fairness